My Classic Stories

The Three Billy Goats Gruff

This book belongs to

Age ------------

Enjoy this book,
love from
The three Billy Goats Gruff

This edition first published in 2013 by Ginger Fox Ltd
Copyright © 2013 Ginger Fox Ltd

Published in the UK by:
Ginger Fox Ltd
Stirling House, College Road
Cheltenham GL53 7HY
United Kingdom

www.gingerfox.co.uk

Retold by Nina Filipek
Illustrated by Bruno Merz

ISBN: 978-0-9557785-8-2

10 9 8 7 6 5 4 3 2 1

Printed and bound in China.

The Three Billy Goats Gruff

Once upon a time there were three billy goats. They were all called Gruff.

One day, the three Billy Goats Gruff set off to look for some fresh grass to eat.

In a meadow on the other side of a river, they saw the best, greenest grass ever.

But to get to the grass they had to cross a bridge over the river.

No one dared to cross the bridge because a *terrible troll* lived under it!

Then the three Billy Goats Gruff had an idea. The little Billy Goat Gruff would go first.

Nervously, he stepped onto the bridge.

Trit-trot, trit-trot, he went.

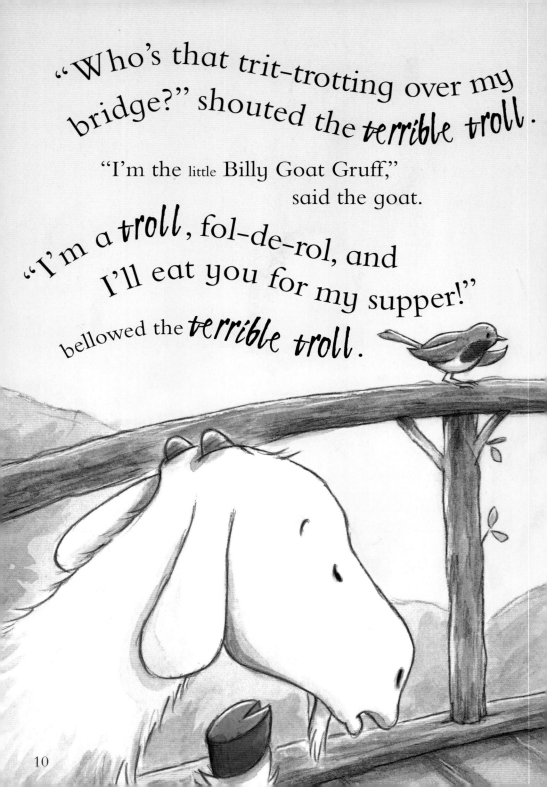

"Who's that trit-trotting over my bridge?" shouted the *terrible troll*.

"I'm the little Billy Goat Gruff," said the goat.

"I'm a *troll*, fol-de-rol, and I'll eat you for my supper!" bellowed the *terrible troll*.

"Please don't eat me. I'm too skinny to eat," said the little Billy Goat Gruff.

"My brother will be here soon. He's bigger than me and much tastier."

The **_terrible troll_** was greedy, so he decided to wait for the **bigger**, tastier goat.

He allowed the little Billy Goat Gruff to
cross the bridge into the meadow
where the best and greenest grass grew.

Next, it was the turn of the middle Billy Goat Gruff. He went slowly trit-trot, trit-trot over the bridge.

"Who's that trit-trotting over my bridge?" shouted the terrible troll.

"I'm the middle Billy Goat Gruff," said the goat.

"I'm a *troll*, fol-de-rol, and I'll eat you for my supper!"

bellowed the *terrible troll*.

"Please don't eat me. I'm too skinny to eat," said the middle Billy Goat Gruff. "My brother will be here soon. He's **bigger** than me and much tastier."

15

Again, the *terrible troll* decided to wait for the **bigger**, tastier goat.

So he allowed the **middle** Billy Goat Gruff to cross the bridge into the meadow where the best and greenest grass grew.

Then it was the turn of the **big** Billy Goat Gruff.

He looked very fierce with his big curved horns and long beard. He went noisily trit-trot, trit-trot then stamp-stomp, stamp-stomp over the bridge.

"Who's that trit-trotting over my bridge?" shouted the *terrible troll*.

"I'm the big Billy Goat Gruff!"

he shouted, louder than the *terrible troll!*

"I'm a *troll*, fol-de-rol, and I'll eat you for my supper!" bellowed the *terrible troll*.

"No you will not!"

BOOMED the big Billy Goat Gruff.
He stamped his hooves on the bridge,

STAMP-
STOMP

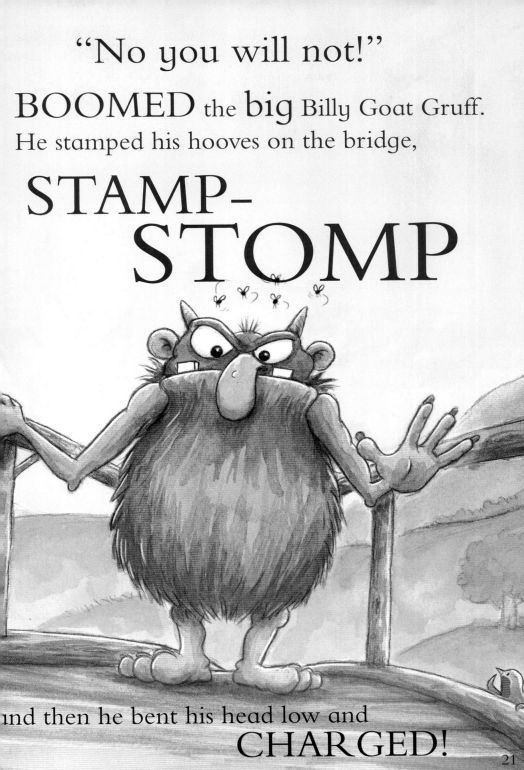

and then he bent his head low and
CHARGED!

The **big** Billy Goat Gruff butted the *terrible troll* with his **big** horns and knocked him straight off the bridge.

The **terrible troll** fell with a huge

splash!

into the
river below.

23

With the *terrible troll* gone, the big Billy Goat Gruff joined his brothers in the meadow where the best and greenest grass grew.

And no one saw the *terrible troll*

ever again!

Now everyone could cross the bridge in safety, and they all lived happily ever after.

Can you remember?

Now that you have read the story, try
to answer these questions about it.

1. How many Billy Goats Gruff were there?

2. What noise did the little Billy Goat Gruff
   make when he crossed the bridge? Was it:

trit-trot,
      trit-trot?   OR   rat-a-tat-tat? ?

3. Which Billy Goat Gruff was the second to go over the bridge?

4. Who fell splash! into the river?

5. Why were the Billy Goats Gruff
   worried about crossing the river?
   Was it because:

   the river was deep?

         OR

   the bridge was broken?

         OR

   a terrible troll lived
   under the bridge?

6. "What
colour is my
fur?"

26

Did you spot?

The *terrible troll* hid under the bridge, but who else was hiding? See if you can find them all.

1. Did you spot the mole in his hole?

2. Can you see the two rabbits in the story?

3. Here is a harder one... Did you see the cricket sitting on a flower?

4. Can you find the two mice sitting on a rock?

5. Did you see the two woolly sheep?

6. The robin appears nine times. Can you find all nine?

True or false?

Can you answer these true or false
questions correctly?

1. The little Billy Goat Gruff had the biggest horns.

   ## True or false?

2. The second Billy Goat Gruff to cross
   the bridge was the little Billy Goat Gruff.

   ## True or false?

3. The three Billy Goats Gruff tricked the *terrible troll*.

   ## True or false?

4. "I'm a *terrible troll!*"
   ## True or false?

5. The middle
   Billy Goat Gruff
   was the first to cross
   the bridge.

   ## True or false?

Such a puzzle ...

Look carefully at the pictures below
and then try to answer the questions.

1. What happens
in this part of the story?

2. What is wrong in this
picture of the *terrible troll*?

Complete your collection ...

"Which one will you read next?"